ELK

DANIEL J. COX

Foreword by Michael Furtman

Chronicle Books
San Francisco

Acknowledgments

I would like to thank the special people of Yellowstone
National Park, especially their Public Affairs Officer,
Ms. Joan Anzelmo. For eleven years she has kindly
assisted me with ideas and direction. Thanks should
also go to the kind and friendly people of western
Canada, who are truly blessed with majestic mountains.

Printed in Hong Kong.

Library of Congress Cataloging in Publication Data

Cox, Daniel J., 1960–
    Elk / Daniel J. Cox ; foreword by Michael Furtman.
        p.   cm.
    ISBN 0-87701-828-6 (pbk.)
    1. Elk—Rocky Mountains Region.   2. Elk—Rocky Mountains Region-
-Pictorial works.   I. Title.
    QL737.U55C68   1992
    599.73′57—dc20   91-24860
                                                              CIP

ISBN 0-87701-828-6
Editor: Carey Charlesworth
Book and cover design: Karen Pike

Distributed in Canada by Raincoast Books, 112 East Third Ave.,
Vancouver, B.C. V5T 1C8

10 9 8 7 6 5 4 3 2 1

Chronicle Books
275 Fifth Street
San Francisco, CA 94103

■

This book is for my grandparents; Selma and Robert Stanford and Jim and Gertrude Cox. Both families were directly responsible for my love and appreciation of the outdoors and its creatures. Also, once again, as always, to my sweet Julie.

Deep stirrings drove the bull elk from the cover of the forest to the edge of the mountain glen. His breath made ghosts in the chilled yellow dawn. His dark shoulders and tawny sides were wet with the morning dew, and the forest behind him glittered with autumn frost.

The bull stomped. Tilting up his black muzzle—laying his splendid, many-tined rack nearly upon his back—he quivered, curled his lips, and discharged a piercing, quavering bugle that culminated in roaring grunts. Standing in the tall, drab grass, the shadowed forest of aspen, spruce, and pine behind him, he ripped the morning air with a calliope of wildness and claimed as his the world around him, forbidding every bull, calling every cow.

Few who have heard the bugled challenge of a bull elk ever forget it; fewer still fail to be stirred by its wild, primal lustiness.

This call is truly ancient. The North American elk, mistakenly labeled by early immigrants from Europe (where "elk" refers actually to what we call "moose") is both old and young; old in its heritage, young for this continent. A member of the genus *Cervus*, of which there are about fifteen species worldwide, the ancestors of the North American elk migrated here across the Bering-Chukchi land bridge, which was exposed during repeated glacial cycles, forming a link between Siberia and Alaska. Though elk certainly moved into North America during earlier glacially induced exposures of this land bridge, their population migrated most widely after the latest, in the Wisconsin glacial stage of ten thousand years ago, and increased with the extinction then of many native fauna.

Evidence that the elk is truly an Old World emigrant exists in its similarity to the Eurasian red deer, and in fact that they are still capable of producing fertile offspring when interbred. Because of this, the elk and red deer are now considered the same species, *Cervus elaphus*, although there are certainly both visible and audible differences. The elk is larger, with a different form to its antlers, and has a high-pitched bugle suited to open spaces rather than the red deer's mating roar, which carries better in its favored forests. In fact, the elk is the most highly evolved member of this genus.

(previous page) During the rut, bulls seek the cover of timber by day and use the mountain meadows and other open areas during the night, early morning, and evening. The high-pitched sound of a bull bugling travels farther in open areas than in the timber.

(left) Bugling is an advertising call for bull elk. It is a challenge to potential rivals who may be nearby. By bugling back and forth, the bulls can locate each other for attack.

After the last ice age, elk gradually expanded their range in North America until they occupied every niche, with the exception of desert, the arctic, and the humid regions of the Southeast. Slowly the populations evolved until, when the Europeans first arrived on these shores, six distinct subspecies of elk occupied most of North America. Enormously adaptable, these subspecies flourished: Tule elk in the California bottomlands; Roosevelt elk in the Pacific Northwest's coniferous rain forests; Merriam elk of the southwestern chaparral mountains; Manitoban elk of the Great Plains; Eastern elk throughout the forests of the East and South; and the Rocky Mountain elk in the rugged western uplands.

Elk were found in every contiguous state and most Canadian provinces. Today, wild elk exist in only twelve states and three provinces. Although no one knows how many elk were present when the settlers first arrived, they probably numbered near ten million and were second only to the bison in count. Agriculture's manipulation of habitat, combined with market slaughter for hides, tusks (canine teeth), and meat, eliminated elk from much of their range. They were not driven into the mountains, as some suggest, but only survived there because of remoteness. Of all the related subspecies of *Cervus elaphus* in the world, only two have become extinct, both of these in the United States. Neither the Eastern nor Merriam elk will ever be seen or heard again, and the Tule elk has barely escaped that sad fate. Of the remaining subspecies, some five to seven hundred thousand currently exist.

Behavior differs between the sexes according to their strategies for successful reproduction. The cow's role in life is to bear and rear calves, and the most effective way for her to do this is in the company of other cows. This herding tendency allows for greater protection, since in a large group there are more eyes, ears, and noses to detect a stalking predator. Even then, should predators strike, the cow and calf's odds of escaping are better because of the large herd size; they are but two targets among many. Feeding is also enhanced by joining a herd, for in order to feed, an elk's head must be down, a distinct disadvantage in spotting a predator. Being in the company of other wary elk allows the cow to depend more on the alertness of others so that she may spend more time feeding, building the reserves that will nurture her calf.

Bull elk have different requirements. In order to attract cows and defeat rival bulls, they must become large and powerful. Their magnificent antlers are an extension of this. To grow such a body and rack, as well as accumulate the fat reserves needed to survive the rigors of the rut, when the bull feeds very little, a bull elk must seek out abundant, high-quality browse. So during most of the snow-free months the bull elk wanders alone, searching for needed browse, depending upon this quiet, solitary lifestyle to build strength and avoid predators. But after the rut the bulls gather in large bands for protection during the winter. A weary bull with depleted reserves from the rigors of the rut would be an easy target among a band of well-conditioned cows, and easy for a predator to spot because of his rack. By forming large bachelor groups the bulls enjoy the same safety in numbers with similarly conditioned herd members that cows do: an effective antipredator strategy. Staying together through much of the winter, the bulls shed their antlers as spring nears. Once this happens, their social structure, which is much influenced by antler size, deteriorates and the bulls struggle to determine dominance. Because such struggles are a waste of energy during a difficult time of year, the wise bull elk again leaves the bachelor group, for more peaceful, productive browsing on his own.

Cows give birth to calves in the months of May and June, the exact dates dependent upon latitude. Most cow elk bear a single calf per year and do so in solitude. Calves are not particularly nimble, even though born quite large (twenty to forty-five pounds), and so upon the warning bark of their mothers they practice a hide and freeze strategy to avoid predators. After two or three weeks they can run (and jump and kick up their heels — they are often very playful) and so mother and calf join other cows and calves in the protective herd. Since the normal antipredator strategy for elk is to run fast and far, thereby outdistancing the predator and leaving the area of danger, calves would be at risk if they entered the herd before being able to keep up with it.

In its first wondrous summer of life, a calf elk lives mostly in the company of other calves. Their "day care

(next page) A bull elk wanders on the shores of the Athabasca River in the Canadian Rockies.

centers" are watched over by a handful of cows, allowing the remaining herd members the chance to feed. Most of the day the calves stay together, but periodically each cow allows her calf (and hers alone) to suckle. Provided they survive their first and most critical winter, the calves continue to grow until they mature sexually. Cows normally do not produce calves until they are at least two years old. Bull elk need about four years to reach sexual maturity, but they are rarely successful at mating until, in seven to twelve years, they have attained a size and stature that will allow them to compete with rival bulls. In most populations an elk that has reached its mid-teens is considered quite old, although some survive into their twenties.

And so the year, except winter, which is geared toward simple survival, revolves around reproduction: the bulls struggle for the size and strength to reproduce; the cows strive to bear and rear a new generation of calves.

Autumn is the most active and dramatic season for elk. As the weather cools, with the leaves on the mountainsides awash in color and the first snows nipping the craggy peaks, the ancient ritual of the mating rut begins. The bulls have grown, polished, and honed their antlers to ivory and mahogany splendor; nearly five months have passed from the time the antlers first sprouted. Once they are dropped in late winter, the cycle resumes almost immediately. As is typical of Old World deer, antlers are formed on a six-point plane and are designed both to catch a rival's rack and to disengage smoothly after sparring. For a bull, antlers are the sign of his dominance, his tool for mastery. And to a cow, they are more than just the bull's most showy attraction, but signify, through the rack's size, that this bull would be a good mate, for he has the skills to have survived to such an age and to find enough food to fuel his large growth.

Because bulls of an age to mate number fewer than sexually mature cows, elk practice a polygamous mating system. In order to gather a harem of cows, the bull must advertise his presence and desirability to them; hence his high-pitched bugling. In essence, the cows choose him, and a bull is sorely tested over the period of the rut by both this vigorous advertisement and the defense of

(left) A cow elk grazes on new grass shoots with her calf.

his harem from other bulls, who seek to depose him. These frantic activities leave him little time to feed, even if his high levels of testosterone and excitement would allow him to do so; the bull depends upon reserves of fat to see him through this exhausting time. Bulls sometimes so deplete their strength during the rut that they enter the frigid, white months in poor condition and succumb to the rigors of winter.

Nothing is more costly to a bull elk than a full-fledged fight for dominance of a harem. Most contests between rivals are limited to short sparring matches to establish hierarchy. Bulls would rather rely upon such matches and a general show of antler size, bugled messages, and posturing to establish rank than fight. Deciding a "winner" this way saves both bulls energy. Occasionally the sparring does develop into an exhausting fight; the thousand-plus-pound bulls, five feet tall at the shoulder, lock antlers. The battle becomes a prolonged shoving match, each powerful bull straining, heaving, and twisting his neck in an effort to drive back or unfoot his rival. Elk antlers are designed primarily as a shield to catch the competitor's rack, but should one bull stumble, the other may quickly disengage and gore his opponent. A combatant that wishes to end the fight unmeshes his antlers and flees. Even then he may be pursued and gored from behind.

As with humans, the winner tends to get the last say. The victorious bull will bark at the defeated rival, and follow that with a triumphant bugle.

Cows do not choose bulls only through such displays of vigor. There is evidence that they respond to kindness and affection, and the experienced courtship of an older bull is therefore often chosen over the fast and rough romance of a young bull. There have been a few rare descriptions of cow elk actually courting a desirable bull. Since the cow is less likely to want to leave such an attentive bull and his gentle treatment, the older, more deliberate bull is further rewarded by having to expend less of his depleting energy reserves in maintaining his harem.

When the frantic rut is over, the elk resume a less harried life, one designed to maximize winter survival. They move into areas of good browse and less snow. Even so,

(previous page) Two mature bulls lock antlers late in August. The serious rut period is still three to four weeks away. Most bulls are content to shove and push each other, using their antlers as a means to lock bodies for the wrestling match.

elk must face one point in the cycle even more inevitable than mating: death. For in the winter death stalks elk in the guise of deep snow and starvation, of frigid weather and weakness, and in the furred form of patient predators. Having planted the seed of new life during autumn, some elk will not live to see its fruition come the warmth of spring. In many areas the herds seek more food and less snow by migrating to lower elevations. When resident on the prairie, elk most likely spend much of the winter in the relative protection of the narrow forest along meandering prairie rivers.

The Shawnee Indians of the plains called the elk *wapiti,* and this animal was also known to virtually every tribe from the mountains of Pennsylvania to the coastal plains of California. Elk were surely hunted even by the early Paleo-Indians of the post-glacial era. From that time until the annihilation of the Indian way of life, elk were important to many tribes. Wapiti were hunted for meat, and the hide was especially treasured, for it is tough and thick and served the natives' needs better than the hide of any other animal for many clothing items, especially cold weather garments and ceremonial wear. Wealthy, as well as lucky, was the individual who had an elk robe, commonly with the fur still intact, for winter wear.

Elk teeth were frequently used as ornaments on clothing and as jewelry. They were the pearls of the prairie and were considered family heirlooms, which signified stature and wealth.

Antlers served as the raw material from which to craft tools. They were finely split to make backing for bows; used as tips for spears and harpoons; made into chisels to shape arrowheads from bone, obsidian, or flint; and carved into spoons, fleshers, plows, and wedges to split firewood.

With such a relationship to elk, it is not surprising that many tribes of the Great Plains and mountains had elk cults and that this revered creature fit into their religious beliefs. For a long time human and elk existed in harmony and respect.

Elk came into serious decline with the coming of the white culture. Elk populations are a mere shadow of those of the past, but for the foreseeable future, elk will continue to have a place in this world. Sound game management,

the protection of habitat, advocacy by groups such as the Rocky Mountain Elk Foundation, and value attributed to elk as both a challenging beast to hunt and a symbol of the wilderness remaining in the West assures that they will be given some due. They have been reintroduced to areas where they once thrived and where habitat yet remains. Still, they face the constant encroachment of humans and the competition of domestic livestock, and they are killed in large numbers by poachers who sell their meat and antlers. (Elk antlers are sold as medicine and an aphrodisiac to an extensive Oriental market.) Especially because their response as prey is to flee, elk are frequently driven from ideal habitat by the increasing network of logging roads and by both recreational and residential developments.

Elk were once more widespread than any species of deer, more even than the familiar white-tail. That seems hard to believe today, and sad, considering what we have lost. No more will the bugle of an elk split the dawn of an Adirondack morning. No more will the milling, grazing herds be seen on the one-time prairie of Iowa or Minnesota, or will a mighty bull grunt and wallow beneath the cottonwoods of some prairie stream.

Serene cow, frisking calf, majestic bull: will they always have a place to carry on those rituals evolved through eons? It is clear that the elk of North America cannot readily adapt when faced with the demands of our society. It is equally clear that for elk to thrive, we must do the adapting, with enough humility to give this ancient race its place on the planet.

The bull elk bugling on the dawn, the cow listening intently to his display, they know nothing of all this, know only that which is contained deep in each cell, the primal urges that direct their actions. Given space, elk will do what elk have always done. And both elk and humans will be richer for it.

(left) A young bull elk ambles through a misty, late summer morning.

19

SPRING

Springtime in the Rockies is truly a misconception. March twenty-first very often passes without so much as a hint of the changing weather elsewhere. Even the perennial spring beauty, a sure sign of the calendar's progress, is scarce to nonexistent at the vernal equinox here in the mountains of the West, where the life cycle of the elk is played out. What spring there is can be suspended on a moment's notice, but when it does take hold, it does so tenaciously.

A spring day in the mountains might bring bright blue skies and temperatures in the sixties for a twelve-hour period. The next few days can be a mix of broken clouds, sleet, sunshine, rain, and sometimes snow. Even so, at a given elevation the genetic clock of the elk ticks on with little or no notice of the weather, and soon the elk cows individually head for more private timber to give birth to their calves, once more starting the loop that ends with death and begins with life.

I was fortunate in witnessing one of spring's challenges to the elk, in this case to a cow and her calf, one day around the first of June. It was one of those days when the clouds blow in and out, covering the warming sun. The wind blew continually and its crispness made me yearn for warmer clothes as I sat at the edge of the swollen river, using my binoculars to watch a herd of cows with recently born calves far across the meadow.

The calves were fairly surefooted, so I was confident that they weren't newborns but at least five to six days old. All that morning I watched as the young ones slept and the cows grazed. Finally, just after noon the calves began to get active, standing up, stretching, and prancing on stiff, spindly legs. It wasn't long before two of the cows began to walk toward me, heading for the far end of the meadow.

As they approached, it became obvious that they would soon have to cross the river to go any farther. How, I thought, can their calves be expected to cross a river that's running powerfully and actually as wide as a small lake, with waters from melting snows. I couldn't imagine such young, seemingly weak creatures navigating it.

(previous page) A calf peeks out from the edge of a spruce forest in early spring.

(left) A bull elk grazes on the fresh new shoots of spring grass while snow gently falls, a reminder of winter just past. The early spring grasses are extremely important to the rejuvenation process. Even elk that make it through the harshest part of winter can die when the snows are mostly finished if the spring thaw is overly late.

A cow elk leads her new calf into a river rushing with snowmelt, to cross a large mountain meadow. She prods him with calls of encouragement, but once in the stream he is swept away, to his own continual calls of distress. She runs along side on the far bank. Finally he is washed close to the riverbank and pulls himself out, tired and frightened. For several hours he just stands on the riverbank, allowing his mother to groom him.

The next morning, the river was lower. The young calf rose from the spot where he had washed up and simply leaped in and swam to his mother, now returned to the other side, upon which they walked off together across the meadow. No harm seemed to have been done.

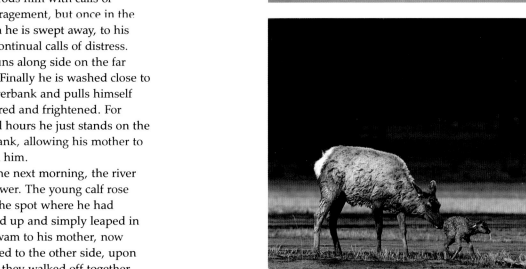

One cow waded into the shallow edge of the river. Actually it was overflow from the main river, water that had spilled over its banks to cover meadow grasses. There was no danger in this part of the river. Just beyond, however, was a different story. As the cow proceeded, the calf obediently followed, its actions a bit jerky and frightened. The cow sank into water up to her belly and the calf continued on, squealing intermittently, obviously distressed. The cow several times looked back, called to her calf, and proceeded; the calf obediently advanced, then hit the faster, deep running water and was immediately swept downstream from its mother. Its cries became louder and more excited and the cow shot across the river, emerging on the bank on the other side. She bolted from the water and ran along the edge of the powerful surging river trying to keep abreast of her calf, now totally out of control and being swept like a leaf on the wind. Amazingly, the calf bobbed like a cork, riding the rushing waters with apparent ease, his pink lips emitting one call after another, and when he finally came to solid ground, his mother was there to meet him.

All of this excitement caught the attention of another cow, one that had already safely crossed, and she too came running to the excited call of the calf. Both mothers sniffed and checked the calf as he wearily pulled himself from the cold waters. When the other cow confirmed he wasn't hers, she left to continue grazing; the calf's mother stayed behind.

All that afternoon I sat and watched the calf as it lay in the grasses just at the river's edge. The small landfall it had swum to was a high piece of ground but actually surrounded by water from the distended river. On three sides he could have walked to drier ground by crossing water up to his knees. On the fourth lay the menace that had washed him to the island in the first place. The daylight ended, and I left thinking that in the wet, soggy grasses, traumatized, he might not make it through the night.

The next morning I arrived rather late. The calf, however, was in the same spot as the day before. His movements showed that he was still alive, to my relief, and shortly after I got there he stood to stretch. There was a cow across the river, the side he had originally come from, and she took notice as the calf stood. She called to her youngster and he answered. The elk talk continued and the calf began to approach the river, now more tame than a day earlier.

With amazingly little hesitation the calf plunged into the waters, swam to the other side, and easily pulled himself onto the bank. His mother greeted him with much licking and affection as he charged forward with urgency and began to nurse. When the young elk finished, they walked off across the meadow in the direction of where the whole ordeal had begun.

Maybe it was just a trial lesson; maybe they can change their minds; one can only speculate as to why the cow acted as she did. One thing is clear, however. Mother nature can be cruel, but a healthy young calf can take a great deal of punishment and live to do it again the next day, only better.

(next page) A young elk cow grazes during an early spring rain.

Cow elk separate themselves from the herd several days before they are to give birth. Once born, the new calf will remain isolated with the cow for what is called the "hiding period," which can last from ten days to three weeks.

(right) A cow elk stands beside the tree she was rubbing against. Hair clings to her lips after she has used her teeth to scratch. With spring's much warmer temperatures, the heavy coats of winter become a tremendous burden and elk spend a great deal of time rubbing their bodies against trees, sometimes using their teeth to remove the shedding coat.

Elk cows with spring calves in sagebrush prairie.

The spots on the back of a calf elk are designed by nature for camouflage. The calf also produces almost no scent, so it is very difficult for predators, such as the coyote, to seek it out and carry it away. This calf is hiding among fallen fire-charred lodgepole pines.

SUMMER

It was a warm summer afternoon, and thunderheads from the plains of southern Idaho pushed across the heavens and threatened to block the sun. Once again showers were coming, their daily arrival now nearly as regular as the hands on a clock. Soon the heat would be squelched. The herd of elk sluggishly dozing in the meadow would come to life once again.

Summer in the Rockies is a lazy time for the creatures living among the mountains and their meadows. The elk spend days moving little more than is required to exist. The calves, however, are an exception. It is during summer that they gain their strength and stamina, acting out games that resemble life-threatening situations they might face later on, as well as acquiring the social skills they need to comfortably fit into the class system within their herd.

I waited among the trees at the edge of the meadow, and as a light drizzle began to fall my lens pointed in the direction of the now-active calves. As predicted, the temperature had dropped considerably and the two-month-old calves were now showing signs of life: rising from their beds, stretching, then looking for a playmate to start the afternoon's antics. As the calves began to cavort I noticed movement as well far in the distance, and it wasn't long before several cows were looking in the same direction. It soon became obvious that whatever it was, the adult elk in the group were growing more concerned, for three cows rose to their feet without taking their eyes off the approaching intruder. I raised my binoculars and found the advancing creature to be a lone coyote. He trotted in the typical bouncing gate, tongue dangling and nose in the air as he moved quickly along.

Twenty minutes passed, and two of the cows had left the herd, walking out across the meadow in the direction of the oncoming coyote. Unaware of the advancing elk, the coyote began to mouse, sticking his head into clumps of grass, perking up his ears, and shooting straight into the air two to three feet to pounce at whatever it was he had heard. At about forty feet the coyote finally noticed the elk and the impending attack. The elk cows charged

(above) Yellow glacier lilies brighten the forest floor of an aspen grove. The elk antler, dropped by a passing bull some three months earlier, will be consumed by the small rodents of the forest, such as mice, porcupines, and squirrels.

(previous page and left) A cow will search for a solitary area to give birth. But once the calf is two to three weeks old, together they will make the journey back to the herd she left.

(next page) It was once thought that settlers' advancement through the West caused the Eastern and Manitoban elk to flee to the Rocky Mountains for security, but it is now understood that they were separate subspecies, adopted to other terrain. The Eastern elk, like the southwestern Merriam, is considered extinct, wiped out by encroaching civilization.

and the coyote took off at full speed, heading for a clump of downed pines for refuge with the elk in close pursuit. The coyote dashed in between two fallen trees; using them as barriers seemed to work, for the cows went around and around the fallen pines looking over the tops to better see the trapped coyote. There he lay for forty-five minutes as the elk circled, trying to figure out how to get at him. I moved in a bit closer to record the dilemma on film and saw his ears were held back, his body in a crouch as the cows moved closer. Obviously, he was in distress.

An hour passed, and the elk finally seemed to be losing interest. The main herd was now close to a half-mile away, and the coyote seemed no longer to be a threat to the calves. Soon they began to head back to the herd, and the coyote slunk out the back side of the logs, keeping his tail between his legs and back lowered as he made his escape.

The coyote was apparently lucky this time, for there are reports of elk ganging up and mobbing a single coyote, killing the animal if he has no escape. The coyote can and does prey on the newborn calves in their early days of life. I have heard of small packs of coyotes taking larger, older calves when given the chance, as well. The coyote is an opportunist, and he will take advantage of any chance he gets that presents a meal. In this case I honestly believe he was simply in the wrong place at the wrong time. The elk made sure he got the message.

(above left) One of the antipredator strategies practiced by the elk on coyotes is called mobbing. Two or more cows gang up to chase a coyote that has gotten too close to the calves. Here they have chased a coyote into a collection of deadfalls, where he has used the downed trees as protection against their attack. He eventually outwaited them, and survived.

(below left) Calves congregate in a mountain meadow. Calves often band together to form their own little herd within the main herd. Several cows will take turns watching the playful and inquisitive youngsters, allowing the rest of the herd to relax and graze.

(left) Elk calves are very playful creatures, but as carefree as they may seem, there are important reasons for their cavorting. A game of tag between two elk calves helps prepare them for the life-threatening games played out with predators. Learning to run, dodge, kick out, buck, and swerve builds their reflexes, muscles, and overall antipredator strategies.

(right) In the early months of life the cow will lick the backside of her calf to stimulate it to defecate, whereupon she ingests what is produced. In survival value, the health risk to the mother is apparently outweighed by the protective value for the calf. By eating the fecal matter, the cow eliminates evidence of the calf, leaving very few clues for a predator to its whereabouts.

(above) A cow elk amid the floral colors of summer grazes on grasses, dandelions, and spring-beauty flowers.

(left) A cow elk chews on an elk thistle plant, which is an early-summer favorite food of not only the elk but grizzlies and black bears. Humans have also found the plant, if not appealing, at least life sustaining.

(right and next page) The growth of antlers is triggered only by the supply of testosterone; thus their absence in the cows. On a large adult male, antlers can develop fully in 130 to 140 days and weigh up to fifty-five pounds. The soft, fuzzy-looking material that appears on them, called velvet, is actually a skin. It covers the antlers and brings blood and nutrients to them as they are growing.

(above left) A young bull with velvet strips hanging from his antlers pauses at the edge of a mountain pond. The velvet strips are all that remain of the soft, fuzzy cover that encased the now-bone-hard antlers. From mid-August to the first of September all bull elk shed their velvet, rubbing the antlers on trees, bushes, tall grasses, or anything they can push on and rub against. Once the velvet removal starts it is complete in a day or two, but the bulls continue to rub and scrape their racks until they are polished and, in the large male, the antler tips become ivory colored.

(above right) A cow elk browses on a flowering serviceberry tree.

(right) A cow elk, shedding her winter coat.

Summer is a very relaxed time for bull elk. They have little more to do than rest and eat while their massive antlers grow. Bulls separate themselves from the cows in the summer and very often will band together in small groups of five to ten animals. As the summer progresses, so does the size of their antlers, and by mid-September they no longer are interested in the company of the bulls with which they spent the summer months.

FALL

The warm days of summer pass quickly, and with their passage, the primeval instincts of the annual rut arise among the bulls of the elk herd. The grasses in the meadows are no longer the lush green of earlier days; instead there are browns mixed with silvers, golds mixed with purples, and some greens mixed with magentas. The landscape has changed its palette, yet the elk continue to graze, oblivious to the onrushing winter.

An astonishing change begins at the middle to end of August. Bulls become easily agitated by the sight of their summer companions, even bulls who have accepted and possibly even sought the company of others in a bachelor group. It starts with the removal of velvet from their antlers, the shedding of the soft fuzzy tissue that produced their bony headgear, and proceeds to gentle sparring, and finally some will lock antlers in serious battle for the right to mate with area cows.

Serious, to-the-death fights are few, and though I've never seen a lethal one, I did witness the full battle ritual, beginning early one morning toward the end of September. As is often the case at this time of year, the Rockies were ablaze with golden aspens in the draws, the air sharp, the grasses caked with frost, and the sky so blue one could only wonder how the heavens could produce such massive concentrations of a single hue. This particular morning I had followed a raging, screaming, hormone-driven bull into a stand of timber. Around midday he lay down to take a break from his theatrics, which included bellowing profusely at another male somewhere in the distance.

The day dragged on and I sat crouched in the dark timber, peering through gnarly crags. The bull knew of my presence and so I kept a respectable distance, having no interest in either spooking or agitating him in any way. Finally, around two hours before sunset, the bull rose from his day bed and began his performance anew. The stage was set, he was well rested from the day's nap, and he had pent-up aggression due to continual screaming challenges from the distant competitor. The day's unseasonable warm temperatures were dropping as fast

(previous page) The antlers of elk serve several purposes. They symbolize rank, ward off opponents, and lock solidly when bulls want a serious wrestling match.

(left) The cool, crisp air of fall is one of many indications that the annual rut or mating season is underway. Here a large, mature bull bugles to a rival bull somewhere in the distance.

A herd bull sniffs the back quarters of a cow who is receptive and ready to breed. Once the bull mounts the cow, the breeding lasts only seconds. Just one very quick thrust shoves the cow forward and out from underneath the bull, after which she will urinate before grazing or going off to lie down.

as the setting sun, and I wondered how cold it would get before they'd settled their differences.

He began to bugle, and immediately at each call the distant bull would answer. I followed him through low swampland for a ways in the direction of the challenger. He paused at the cool mud of the wet bog, to wallow. First he urinated on the spot, then racked the soggy terrain with his antlers until he broke through the grasses. Minutes passed. Finally his legs buckled, dropping his massive body solidly into the depression he had made in the tarry soil. He began to roll, kicking wildly, stopping now and again to vocally threaten the bull beyond the timber.

After about thirty minutes in the bog, suddenly he had had enough. Jumping to his feet he once again bugled into the setting sun, dripping with water and caked with mud. I remember the hair on my neck tingling and shivers running down my spine, for what presented itself I can only describe as the bull from hell, freshly risen from the depths of the earth, standing there dripping, black ooze rolling down his withers as he shrieked the challenge again and again.

Once more he advanced, and soon, across the meadow, the challenger appeared, head back, screaming the combination of high-pitched whistle and low guttural grunts that signifies the mating season is in full swing. They made eye contact, both rushed across the hundred yards of meadow—and suddenly their intensity was recast, for as they closed the distance each one pulled up short. With only twenty-five feet between them, they turned broadside to each other, heads held back, tipping their massive antlers from side to side as they followed the lines of an imaginary circle. The ritual had gone one step further; they were now sizing each other up before deciding to actually lock antlers.

In most situations this is as far as a fight will go between two challengers. Usually one of the bulls gets the message that the other is larger, meaner, or more agile and decides to vacate the premises. If not, soon . . . crash! Antlers lock, branches break, small pines are

(previous page) A young bull, less dominant than another not seen in the photo, runs frantically through the harem of cows the dominant bull has gathered. He is running at the cows in sexual frustration as well as away from the dominant bull, who is intent on driving him out of the area.

58

mowed over, and eight massive legs hurl competing bodies in forward thrusts. Attached to the heads of those bodies are nature's daggers, rock hard, polished to white points and easily sharp enough to puncture any hide blocking the path to the sensitive, life-giving organs.

The circular dance of intimidation lasted only moments, and in the blink of an eye the bulls charged, their antlers locked in battle. The two shoved at each other for no more than five furious minutes, and much quicker than it began, it ended; the devil bull fled as fast as his earthly legs could take him. With the competitor gone, the winner was able to regather his cows, once more attending to his herd.

The sun had set, and off to the east I could see the first stars just beginning to shine. The stage-set meadow was now hazy with ground fog, and I hiked through it back to my truck. The curtain dropped across the Montana rockies.

(next page, above) A bull rests during a midday break from the frenzied rut. When elk are calves they are preyed upon by black bears, grizzly bears, coyotes, wolves, mountain lions, and other predators. But a large, healthy adult elk like this one has little reason to fear.

(next page, below) A large, mature bull rolls and bugles in a wallow he's made in a low, wet area of a mountain meadow. Wallowing advertises his presence to cows and other bulls in the area. This behavior is observed mainly in large bulls, but even the cows and yearlings will take advantage of a wallow at times.

(previous page) Typically after making a wallow the bull lies down in it, rubbing his neck and antlers over the urine-soaked ground. Urine marking often accompanies bugling, which leads to the possibility that a dominant bull has a stronger scent than others because he marks himself more, the frequency of his advertisement increasing the intensity of his odor.

(left) Young bull elk battle on winter range.

(left) A bull pauses with his harem of cows.

(next page) A spring calf browses on the leaves of a bush. Whether it will live through its first winter depends on two major factors; its own physical condition and age, as winter descends, and how severe the season will be.

(previous page, above) A cow and her calf born that spring browse on the still-green leaves of early fall. The calf will remain with its mother until the next May or June. At that time the cow will aggressively run it off so as to leave the herd and give birth to another calf alone.

(previous page, below) A calf seems curious about the black-billed magpie on its mother's back. It is probably feeding on parasites; elk can have a number of different external ones, the most common being the winter tick. They can seriously affect the elks health.

(right) Two young bulls prepare to spar. Seldom does a serious battle erupt between bulls of their age.

WINTER

inter in the Rocky Mountains can arrive early, stay late, and produce nearly summerlike temperatures and then a descent to thirty degrees below zero. The climate is so continually diverse that it's hard to get used to. With such radical changes in temperature plus accumulations of deep snow, stress increases; elk and other animals of the mountains become more susceptible to the elements. It is during the winter and the similarly fluctuating weather of early spring that elk are at particular risk.

Large winterkills are not a common occurrence in Montana, and during the two years I worked with the elk I encountered only three carcasses of animals that had succumbed to nature's forces. Studies of which animals are most affected by severe weather pinpoint the younger and older ones; specifically, calves and mature bulls are most likely to die from a harsh winter. Prime-aged cows, those with the most potential for repopulating the herds, are most resistant.

In the winter of 1989–1990 a large winterkill did occur in the Yellowstone National Park area. There, 24 to 27 percent of the herd died, due to a combination of factors. To begin with, the available forage was inadequate. Record numbers of bison and deer as well as the elk arrived on their winter range several weeks earlier than normal. It is believed they came early due to that year's destruction by fire of vegetation, and the drought conditions on their summer range. With such a high concentration of elk on their wintering grounds the range conditions rapidly deteriorated, and soon thousands of elk were feeling the effects of a harsh winter, scarce food sources, and too many animals competing for what food was available. Most of the elk that died did so in a rather small time frame, from approximately February seventh to March first. The creeks and river bottoms of the mountains surrounding the northern Yellowstone winter range were dotted with the carcasses of over fifteen hundred elk.

As harsh as it may seem, death for one is surely a blessing for another. Not only does winterkill eliminate the less healthy elk, strengthening the herd, but the

(previous page) An adult bull, one antler already dropped, walks along the river bank in his constant pursuit of food. Other bulls rest. After the stress of the fall rut, some bulls will not make it through the winter and will become a different part of the food chain, sustaining life for those animals, such as the coyote, who depend on dying elk.

(left and next page) Elk feed on a continual basis, to produce enough energy for normal, everyday body functions. During winter storms they may have to fast, as males do during the rut. At these times, the body fat they have stored is used as fuel. Elk forage in winter on stream banks of relatively warm, fast-flowing rivers where grasses may grow all year long, providing essential food sources for many individuals. Natural springs flowing with warm waters from within the earth also provide good grazing areas.

(above) This bull paws at the snow, working to get at the grasses that lie underneath. If the snow gets deeper than sixteen to twenty-eight inches the elk will search for other food sources, such as woody plants and arboreal lichens, changing their feeding habits from grazing to browsing.

(below left) This bull is feeding on the bark of a fallen lodgepole pine tree. His right antler is missing, which is a normal occurrence for this time of year. Winter is the time when all energy is directed toward staying alive; the antlers used for fighting and intimidating other bulls during the fall rut are no longer necessary, so via its hormone cycle the body dispatches them.

(right) Coyote feeding on carcass of winter-killed elk.

whole food chain and scavengers in particular benefit greatly from the selected animals' demise. Birds, coyotes, bears, and others depend heavily on the carcasses they find in the spring and early summer. If it weren't for the food that the weaker elk provide others, many more creatures would weaken, and fall behind their fellows, and eventually the circle of life, one animal depending on the other, would be broken.

As I mentioned earlier, during two years of working with these beautiful animals, only three times did I find the extant carcass of an elk. One of these occasions allowed me to photograph a coyote feeding on the remains of a yearling cow. Amazingly, only the day before I found the carcass I had passed the same area late in the afternoon, and there was no elk. The next morning I arrived to find a yearling cow almost completely consumed, only the hide and skeleton remaining, with small chunks of meat attached to the bones. From prior experience I knew that even these would soon no longer exist, and only millions of individual hairs would remain, scattered over a wide radius in the snow.

(above) This calf is not yet a year old, though its coloration is the same as an adult cow's. The camouflaging protective spots have disappeared. Beneath the outer coat is another layer of hair called the undercoat, which is the single most important factor for retaining body heat in the winter.

(left) The hormone testosterone is directly responsible for this bull's loss of an antler. After the rut, the levels of testosterone within the bull elk begin to drop. When they reach a certain level, a new antler cycle begins with the shedding of the old pair.

(previous page and left) Elk migration depends on one factor: the depth of snow that has accumulated on the summer and fall range. Once the snow depth exceeds one and a half to two feet, the elk begin moving to areas with less. Generally their migration will stop once they have found south-facing windswept slopes and will not continue unless these slopes too become covered.

This cow and her calf are being followed by a young bull who may be the cow's offspring from the previous year. It is a yearling, but its antlers have several branches. Usually the antlers of a yearling bull are only spiked, meaning straight and branchless; yearling bulls with branched antlers are known to occur in very healthy populations.

(left and next page) These elk, on the National Elk Refuge, feed below the Grand Teton Mountains near Jackson Hole, Wyoming.

Prior to the arrival of Europeans, there were perhaps ten million elk in North America. By 1907, fewer than a hundred thousand elk existed and the numbers were dropping. The abrupt and continual decline of elk numbers once white hunters and settlers arrived was finally recognized by the Benevolent and Protective Order of Elks, who were major consumers of the elk tusks for decorative purposes. The B.P.O.E., commonly known as the Elks, initiated a study in 1908 and made recommendations for the species' protection. In 1912 and 1913, fifty thousand dollars was appropriated by Congress to buy 1,760 acres of private land, which it combined with an additional 1,000 acres of public land to create the National Elk Refuge outside of Jackson Hole, Wyoming. In 1925 The Izaak Walton League purchased and donated an additional 1,760 acres, and in 1935 more private land was purchased to bring the total refuge size to 24,700 acres. If it were not for the establishment of this refuge, many believe the Rocky Mountain elk would have been eradicated from their range.

Photographer's Biography

Daniel J. Cox is an internationally published wildlife photographer who has published five other books prior to *Elk* including *Black Bear* (Chronicle Books). He is a regular contributor to the publications of such respected organizations as the National Geographic Society, the Audubon Society, and the Sierra Club, as well as such magazines as *Field and Stream, National Wildlife* and *International Wildlife.* His work has been exhibited at the prestigious Nikon House in New York City. In 1990 he was an award winner in the portrait division of the British Broadcasting Corporations Wildlife Photographer of the Year contest.

Daniel and Julie, his wife and full-time business partner, live in the Rocky Mountains of Montana.

Bibliography

Murie, Olaus J. *The Elk of North America.* Jackson, Wyoming. Teton Bookshop. 1979.

Wildlife Management Institute, *Elk of North America: Ecology and Management.* Harrisburg, Pennsylvania. Stackpole Books, 1982.